SMITHMARK

Copyright © 1992 Kidsbooks Inc. and Michael Teitelbaum
Illustrations Copyright © Renee Grant, *There's Something Weird In That Cave!*;
Barbara Steadman, *There's No Such thing As A Ghost... Is There?*
and *Don't Be Afraid Of the Dark!*; Pat Stewart, *Did You Hear Something?*

Kidsbooks Inc.
7004 N. California Ave.
Chicago, IL 60645

This edition published in 1992 by SMITHMARK Publishers Inc.,
16 East 32nd Street, New York, NY 10016

SMITHMARK books are available for bulk purchase for sales promotion and premium use.
For details write or telephone the Manager of Special Sales. SMITHMARK Publishers Inc.,
16 East 32nd Street, New York, NY 10016. (212) 532-6600.
Manufactured in the United States of America.

SLIGHTLY SPOOKY STORIES™

Did You Hear Something?

Written by
Michael Teitelbaum

Illustrated by
Pat Stewart

In the small town of Beaver Falls, the school wilderness club was having its annual camping weekend. The five regular members of the club were going, along with five campers from a nearby town.

Mr. Terry, the teacher in charge of the club, was leading the campers into the woods.

"Looks like we have a few more kids than last year," said eight-year-old Becky, president of the club.

"Yeah," said nine-year-old Troy, the club's vice-president, with a devilish gleam in his eye. "The more kids, the better the scary story is!"

After about two hours of hiking, the group finally reached the Beaver Falls campsite.

"This is it, gang!" yelled Becky. "We're here!"

Everyone was glad to stop hiking and take off their packs. With Mr. Terry's help, the children took the next hour to set up their tents.

Dinner was cooked over an open campfire, and soon the tired campers had slipped into their tents for the night.

At least, that was what they thought!

When the full moon had risen to its peak in the night sky and he was sure that Mr. Terry was asleep, Troy slipped over to Becky's tent. "Ready?" he whispered.

"Yep," answered Becky. "Let's get the others."

Troy and Becky went from tent to tent, quietly waking the other campers. Soon, all the kids were in Troy's tent—the tent that was farthest from Mr. Terry.

"Are you going to tell us a scary story?" asked seven-year-old Kyle, who loved scary stories.

"I'm going to tell you the Legend of Beaver Falls," began Troy. "Legend has it that something weird lives out in these woods!"

Nervous laughter spread through the tent, as campers huddled close together.

Troy continued. "Late at night, deep in the woods, it is said that you can hear the sounds of a strange creature. This mysterious creature has three legs, huge wings, and makes an eerie, high-pitched, whistling sound. Anyone who has ever heard these sounds will never forget them!"

The sound of footsteps interrupted Troy.
"Did you hear something?" asked Kyle.
The footsteps came again. *Step, step, step,* then a pause. *Step, step, STEP!* and again a pause. Then, one more time, the three-step pattern was repeated.

Next, a high-pitched whistle filled the air, followed closely by the flapping of wings.

"The creature!" whispered Kyle.

Troy and Becky looked at each other. This story had been told in Beaver Falls for years. Becky first heard it from her older brother. But it was just a story. No one had ever really heard the sounds. They were just trying to have a little fun, and keep the legend alive.

But now, Troy and Becky were scared themselves!

"Come on, Troy," said Becky, mustering all her courage. "Let's go check this out."

"Everybody stay here," ordered Troy. "It's okay. Mr. Terry is sleeping right over in that tent. If you see anything, wake him up."

Becky and Troy made their way through the dense, dark woods, guided only by the narrow beams of their flashlights.

Suddenly Becky heard a twig snap behind her and felt a hand grab her shoulder.

"Yaaaa!" she yelled, turning in shock.

There stood Kyle. "Sorry," he said sheepishly. "I didn't mean to frighten you. I just love scary stuff, and I didn't want to miss out on the fun, so I followed you."

Becky caught her breath, and the three children moved on into the woods.

"Did you hear something?" asked Becky a short while later.

Step, step, step, came the sounds. Then a whistle and the flapping of wings.

"It's behind us!" shouted Troy, dashing away from the sounds.

"Troy, it's following us!" cried Becky. Every turn they made, the creature was right behind them.

"We're lost!" exclaimed Troy.

"Lost in the woods with that thing after us!" cried Kyle. The sounds came again, and the children kept running.

They came upon a clearing in the woods. There, in the middle of the clearing, stood a log cabin. Smoke curled from its chimney.

"It looks like someone's home!" said Becky, fighting back the panic.

"Come on," said Troy. "Maybe we can get some help in there!"

The three campers burst into the cabin, out of breath, and slammed the door behind them. There, sitting peacefully near a blazing fireplace, was an old man.

"Mister, you've got to help us!" cried Troy nervously.

"Yeah," continued Kyle, "there's a creature in the woods chasing us. He's headed this way!"

"Have a seat," the old man said calmly.

"But you don't understand," said Becky excitedly. "There's a creature with three legs and big wings and—"

"Whoa, whoa," interrupted the old man, raising his wrinkled hand. "Slow down, young lady. I assure you there's nothing to be afraid of."

There was no sound outside now except for the forest crickets. The three campers sat down and began to relax.

"Who are you?" asked Becky.

"Well, you might call me a nature lover," began the old man. "For the past 50 years I've lived in the woods. I grow food and flowers, and I've made friends with many of the animals."

The man got up, grabbed his heavy wooden cane and walked to the door. *Step, step, STEP!* he went.

"There's your creature!" said Troy in an excited whisper. "His cane makes the third step."

"I'd like you to meet a friend of mine," said the man. He opened his door and whistled.

"The whistle!" whispered Becky.

A few seconds later they heard the flapping of wings. A big owl came flying over to the old man, landing right on his arm.

"There's your terrible winged creature!" said Becky a bit too loudly.

"I'm afraid that Hooter here is the only terrible winged creature you'll find in these woods," said the old man. "I'm sorry if he frightened you."

The three campers were embarrassed. They told the man about the legend. He let out a big laugh.

"People are always afraid of what they don't understand," he said. "So you came here in search of a terrible creature, huh? Well, I'm sorry to disappoint you."

"No, sir," said Becky. "We're not disappointed. It's very nice to meet you, but we should be getting back to our camp. The others will start to worry."

"I'd rather the whole world didn't find out about my little cabin here," said the old man.

"Don't worry," said Troy. "Your secret is safe with us."

"I'm pretty tired," said the old man. "I'm going to turn in for the night. But come back and visit some time," he added, waving goodbye.

The three campers disappeared into the woods, heading back to their camp.

Back at camp, the others were frantic with worry. Becky, Troy, and Kyle burst from the trees scaring the daylights out of most of the campers.

"What did you find?" everyone wanted to know, as they gathered around the three returning campers.

"Well," began Becky, "we caught a glimpse of the creature, but it darted off into the woods before we could get close enough for a really good look."

"Did it have three legs?" asked one camper.

"And big, ugly wings?" asked another.

"We think so," answered Troy. "But we may never know. Now, I think we should all go to sleep. The creature won't bother us anymore tonight." Troy felt good that he not only kept the legend alive, but was able to protect his new friend's privacy, as well.

As the campers stretched out in their tents, the sound of footsteps once again broke through the night.

Troy dashed to Becky's tent. "Did you hear something?" he asked.

Before she could answer, the unmistakable *Step, Step, STEP!* followed by the whistling and flapping of wings caused heads to pop out of all the tents in camp.

"If the old man is sleeping in his cabin," started Troy.

"Then who's making that noise?" finished Becky.

All the campers, including Troy and Becky, slipped back into their tents, zipping the flaps tightly, and hiding deep inside their sleeping bags.

What they didn't see was an old woman, the old man's wife, walking past their camp. She too walked with a heavy wooden cane, and whistled to call the pet owl she shared with her husband.

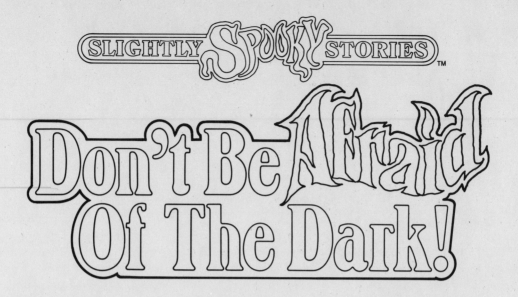

SLIGHTLY SPOOKY STORIES ™

Don't Be Afraid Of The Dark!

Written by
Michael Teitelbaum

Illustrated by
Barbara Steadman

It was a very big night for ten-year-old Lauren and her seven-year-old sister, Dana. Their parents were going out to visit some friends. This was going to be the first time that the two sisters would be left alone for the evening, without a babysitter.

"Remember, we're not going far," said their mother. "It's only about a 15-minute drive."

"And the phone number where we'll be is right there on the kitchen table," added their father. "So if anything happens—"

"Come on, Mom, Dad," said Lauren. "It's not like we're babies. You guys are more nervous than we are!"

"Yeah," added Dana. "We'll be okay. After all, what can happen?"

Lauren and Dana watched as their parents pulled out of the driveway. They stood at the front door waving, then went back into the house.

"So what do you want to do?" asked Dana.

"Let's get a snack and watch some TV," answered Lauren.

The two sisters settled down on the living room floor with a big bowl of popcorn, and turned on the tube.

"I'm glad we don't have a babysitter," said Dana, a short while later. "It makes me feel very grown up!"

"Me too," replied Lauren.

Just then, they heard a loud clap of thunder. They rushed to the window and saw that it had started to rain.

"I didn't know it was supposed to rain tonight," said Lauren, a bit nervously.

"Maybe it will stop in a few minutes," said Dana, hopefully.

But the storm got worse and worse. The rain poured down in sheets. Thunder boomed and lightning flashed. The girls huddled together under a blanket near the window and anxiously watched the storm.

Suddenly, the biggest lightning flash of all lit up the night sky. The next thing the girls knew, the house was dark.

Dana grabbed Lauren's arm and screamed, "What happened!"

"The storm must have knocked out some power," answered Lauren. "Let's go check upstairs. Maybe the lights work up there."

"Lauren, I'm scared," cried Dana.

"Come on, Dana," said Lauren. "Don't be afraid of the dark! It can't hurt you."

Lauren held Dana's hand and started to walk from the living room. As they stepped into the hallway, a flash of lightning caused a huge shadow to appear on the wall. It looked like the shadow of a tall monster with six arms.

"Yikes!" shrieked Dana when she saw the shadow. "A monster!" She dashed up the stairs with Lauren following close behind.

"Try the light switch, Lauren," shouted Dana when they had reached the top of the stairs. Lauren flipped the switch but no lights came on.

"The power in the whole house must be out!" said Lauren. She was getting a bit scared herself. "Let's go get the flashlight!"

They went into their parent's bedroom, where they knew their dad kept a flashlight. But when they flipped it on, nothing happened.

"The batteries must be dead!" cried Lauren.

"Let's go into our bedroom," suggested Dana. She thought that maybe being in their own room would be less scary.

They were sitting together on Dana's bed when Lauren glanced outside. Lightning lit up something just beyond their bedroom window. It was taller than the house, and had gnarled limbs covered with cracked, crusty skin. The thing seemed to be reaching toward their bedroom window and them!

"It's a huge, nasty witch!" screamed Lauren. "Run!"

Dana almost ran over her big sister as the two flew down the stairs.

"Let's call Mom and Dad!" cried Dana. They rushed into the kitchen and Lauren picked up the phone. There was no dial tone.

"The phone is out!" screamed Lauren. "The storm must have knocked down the phone lines, too. We can't call Mom and Dad!"

"Maybe they got worried when they saw the storm, and they're on their way home," wished Dana. "Flip on the radio. Let's see how long the storm is supposed to last."

Lauren turned on a battery-powered radio and put on the news station. "Once again," began the announcer, "we report that due to the storm, all local roads are flooded. Please do not attempt to drive!"

"The roads are flooded," said Dana, growing more scared by the minute. "We're all alone, and Mom and Dad can't reach us!"

"Don't be afraid of the dark," Lauren said again, trying to calm Dana down. "There's nothing here that can hurt us." Holding hands, the two sisters walked into the dining room.

"What's that?" screamed Dana, when they entered the room. There, on the dining-room wall, was the shadow of an ugly, hairy beast!

"It's a horrible creature," yelled Lauren. "And it's in the dining room!"

The girls rushed from the dining room. As they passed the back porch, lightning flashed through the porch windows, and the shadow of a huge insect moved back and forth on the wall.

"It's a giant spider!" cried Dana. "And it's moving!"

The girls were now terrified. They hid under their blanket in the living room, repeating, "Don't be afraid of the dark," over and over to each other.

Just then, the lights in the house came back on. Lauren and Dana threw off the blanket and jumped up and down, shouting "Yaaay! Yaaay!"

"It's a lot less scary with the lights on," said Lauren.

"But what was all that stuff we saw?" asked Dana.

The sisters walked around the house, looking for all the creatures that had scared them in the dark.

"Look!" said Lauren. "That six-armed monster was just the coat stand. The hooks on it looked like arms when its shadow hit the wall."

They ran upstairs to their bedroom. "That witch was just the big old oak tree outside our window," explained Dana. "But it sure looked scary in the dark!"

Back down in the dining room they discovered that the ugly hairy beast was just a large houseplant that cast a scary shadow on the wall.

"What about the big spider?" asked Dana. They stepped out onto the back porch and saw that the rain had stopped and the storm had passed.

"That spider was just the shadow from Mom's old rocking chair," said Lauren. "The wind from the storm made it rock back and forth, so the shadow moved, too."

"Girls! Girls, where are you?" called a voice from the front door.

"It's Mom and Dad!" Lauren and Dana shouted together. "They're home!"

"Is everything all right here?" asked their Dad when the girls came into the hallway. "We heard that the lights were out in the whole town."

"Everything's fine, Dad," said Lauren calmly.

"We had to wait for the storm to pass before we could drive home," said their Mom.

"You two weren't afraid in the dark, were you?" asked their Dad.

"Who, us?" replied Dana, winking at Lauren. "Nah! No way!" They were both feeling very grown up having made it through their first evening alone in the house.

As the girls went upstairs to go to bed, the storm picked up again. Lightning flashed outside their bedroom window. The light coming through the window lit up a shape in the corner of the room. It had a fat gray body, whiskers, and a long tail.

"Look!" cried Dana, pointing to the corner. "A giant rat!" The girls ran screaming from their room.

Lauren and Dana slept with their Mom and Dad that night.
If they had gone back into their room, they would have seen that
the rat they thought they saw was really a large stuffed squirrel
which looked so strange in the eerie light from the storm. The
lovable stuffed toy had fallen from a shelf, and was lying in a corner
of their room.

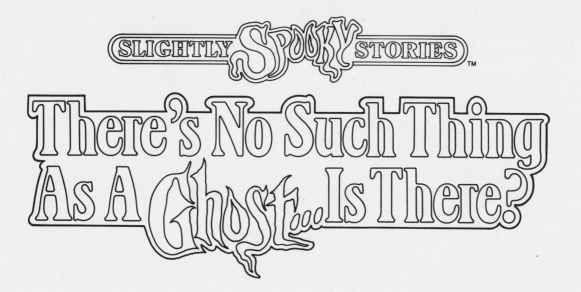

SLIGHTLY SPOOKY STORIES ™

There's No Such Thing As A Ghost....Is There?

Written by
Michael Teitelbaum

Illustrated by
Barbara Steadman

RIIING! RIIING! the school bell rang. A steady stream of happy kids ran out the door and into the schoolyard.

Rachael, Jesse, and Sara Reed had just finished their first day at their brand new school, in their brand new neighborhood.

"Hi, Rachael!" shouted Jesse, as he ran over to his big sister. "How'd it go?"

"Pretty well," she replied. "I met some nice kids. They have a neighborhood club, and they invited us to join."

"Join what?" said Sara, as she joined the others. Rachael explained about the club to her little sister.

Just then, Jackie, the leader of the club came over. "Hey, Rachael," said Jackie.

Rachael introduced Sara and Jesse to Jackie.
"So," said Jackie. "Are you ready for the test to join the club?"
"Test?" asked Rachael.

Jackie explained that on the outskirts of town, there was an old, abandoned mansion.

"All the kids in town know that this big old house is haunted," continued Jackie. "All new members of the club have to spend an afternoon in the haunted house. That's your test to join the club!"

"But what if it's scary?" asked Jesse.

"Well," said Jackie, "it may be. But those are the rules of the club."

Rachael, Jesse, and Sara were frightened. But they really wanted to fit into their new neighborhood and new school. So, they agreed to spend the afternoon in the haunted house.

The Reed kids, along with Jackie and a few other members of the club rode their bikes to the outskirts of town. There, they saw the creepy old mansion.

"Yikes!" said Sara. "That place really does look haunted."

Jackie and the other club members led the three newcomers to the front door of the house.

"Are you going to go through with it?" asked Jackie.

"Yes," said Rachael, trying her best to be brave. She slowly walked up the squeaky front steps. Then she opened the door and walked in, followed closely by Sara and Jesse. Inside, the house was all dusty and creepy. Cobwebs hung from every corner, and scary shadows danced on every wall.

"This isn't so bad," whispered Jesse, as he huddled close to his sisters.

Suddenly they heard a ghostly howl! *AOOOWWW!*

"What was that?" shouted Rachael.

"I was going to ask *you*!" said Jesse.

"There's no such thing as a ghost . . . is there?" asked Sara.

"Of course not," said Rachael. "Let's go find out what that noise was."

Just then, water started running somewhere in the house . . . then just as quickly, stopped.

They headed up the creaky old stairs. As they reached the top of the staircase they heard a door slam.

"GHOSTS!" all three shouted, running back down the stairs as fast as they could. When they reached the first floor they heard the sound of pounding footsteps on the staircase behind them.

"They're after us!" shouted Jesse. "Let's get out of here!"

"Look," yelled Sara. "I see a candle flickering in the next room!"

"No, wait!" insisted Rachael. "I think something fishy is going on here!"

At that very moment, Rachael heard some giggling coming from outside a nearby window. "Shh!" warned Rachael. "Listen." Suddenly the shutters on the window began to bang against the side of the house.

"I think I know what's going on here," said Rachael. "You two wait here. And don't be scared. It's all right. I'll be close by."

Rachael slipped out the front door of the house and snuck around to the window. There, she saw Jackie and a couple of the other kids from the club moving the shutters and giggling.

"So it *was* them," she said to herself. "They were making all the noises. I think I'll teach them a little lesson."

Rachael crept up behind them very quietly and then yelled in her loudest voice, "BOO!"

The kids from the club all shrieked in fright and jumped at the sound.

"GOTCHA!" shouted Rachael.

"You scared us half to death!" said Jackie. Then they all cracked up, laughing. When Sara and Jesse heard the laughter from inside the house, they came running out to join the others.

"What I don't understand," began Rachael, "is how you moved around the house without being seen."

"That's easy," replied Jackie, as he led everyone back inside. "This old mansion has lots of secret doors and passageways. We've been playing in here for years, so we know most of them pretty well."

"Then there really are no ghosts?" asked Sara.

"No, of course not," said Jackie. "Welcome to our club!"

OOOOOH!
Suddenly, a loud, eerie howl came from somewhere deep inside
the house.
"Come on," said Rachael. "The joke's over."

Jackie looked at the other club members.

"*We're* all here . . ."

Rachael looked at Sara and Jesse. "And *we're* all here . . ."

"THEN WHO IS DOING THAT HOWLING?" they all shouted together as they ran at top speed from the house.

Nobody even dared to look back as they ran.

If they had looked back, they would have seen a cute little dog trot out of the house, waging its tail and howling at the top of its lungs!

SLIGHTLY SPOOKY STORIES™

There's Something Weird In That Cave!

Written by
Michael Teitelbaum

Illustrated by
Renee Grant

Sean Daniel and his big brother Adam were on vacation with their parents. They were on their way into a hotel, on a tropical island. "Why do they call this 'Voodoo Island?'" Adam asked his father. "Is there real voodoo magic on this island?"

"There sure is," came a voice from behind them. It was a native of the island. "Strange and powerful magic can be found in the caves on Voodoo Island. You must be careful!"

"I want to go check out the Voodoo Caves!" exclaime[d]
Sean when they arrived at their hotel room.

"Yeah!" added Adam. "It sounds great to me."

The Voodoo Caves were part of the hotel complex. Th[e]
tourist attraction provided some local flavor and fun f[or]
hotel visitors.

"I guess we're going to the Voodoo Caves today!" sa[id]
the boys' father, smiling.

That afternoon, Sean, Adam, and their parents went to visit the Voodoo Caves. At the entrance to the caves, a guard pointed the family in the right direction.

"Be careful," said the guard. "There are many tricky turns in there."

The family stepped into a dark, eerie cave. Sean and Adam ran ahead and soon found themselves separated from their parents. They came to a sign that said "North Tunnel," and continued wandering through the cave's twisting, turning passageways.

Soon the two brothers came to a large cavern. Smoke filled the huge underground room, and the boys' footsteps echoed strangely on the damp stone floor.

Then, suddenly, something moved among the smoke and shadows.

"What's that?" shouted Sean, pointing straight ahead.
A figure appeared. He was small, and dressed in the costume of a voodoo chief. Brightly-colored feathers and rattling bones made up a belt that sat around his waist. His bare chest was covered with colored paints. On his head he wore a voodoo mask that was carved into a frightening expression.

"Who are you?" asked Adam. He was scared, but was trying not to let it show.

Without a word, the strange figure turned and disappeared back into the smoke.

"Let's get out of here!" said Sean to his older brother.

"No, wait," said Adam bravely. "The cave goes on from here, let's see if we can find that voodoo guy."

The boys crept deeper into the cave. The passageway narrowed and then opened into a large room. In the center of the room stood an old statue. It looked like a tall version of the voodoo chief they had just seen.

"Look at the expression on his face," said Sean, pointing to the statue's carved, wooden head.

"He has a really creepy smile," added Adam, who was starting to feel kind of creepy himself. "Let's get out of here!"

The boys retraced their steps, and soon found their parents.

"Wait until we tell you what we saw!" exclaimed Sean as they rambled on about the little man and the strange statue.

"That statue could be thousands of years old," explained their dad, back at the hotel. "Or it could just be something put there to amuse the tourists on the island."

"But what about that little voodoo guy?" asked Sean.

"It was probably just your imagination, honey," said his mom.

But both Sean and Adam knew that they had seen someone or something moving in that cave.

The next day, Adam and Sean wanted to return to the mysterious
cave.

"Don't you want to go to the beach with us?" asked their mom.

"We really want to solve this mystery," said Adam. "Please?"

"Well," said their mom. "I guess it's okay. The cave *is* part of the
hotel complex. You two just make sure that the guard knows where
you are!"

Sean and Adam ran back to the cave.

"You kids back for another look?" asked the guard.

"Yes, sir," said Adam. "We want to go back down the North Tunnel."

The guard nodded, and the brothers started into the cave. They soon reached the smokey cavern they had visited the day before. Once again the strange figure stepped from the smoke. This time he pointed toward the large room that contained the statue. Then he disappeared from sight.

"I'm scared," said Sean. "There's something weird in that cave! I just know it!"

"Come on," said Adam boldly. "Let's go find out what it is that he wants us to see!"

The boys made their way through the narrow passageway that led into the large cavern. There stood the voodoo statue, only now its face was sad and frowning, not smiling!

"Voodoo magic!" shouted both boys as they went running from the cave.

"Mom! Dad!" shouted Adam breathlessly as the boys ran up to their parents at the hotel's beach.

"Slow down, guys," said their mother. "What's going on?"

"The voodoo magic in that cave we told you about!" cried Sean. "It's real. The face on the statue changed!"

"And we saw that little voodoo guy again!" added Adam.

"Come on guys," said their father. "You don't really believe that voodoo stuff, do you?"

"There's something weird in that cave," said Adam, "and we'll prove it to you! Come on, Sean, let's get my camera, go back to the cave, and get a picture of that voodoo guy!"

The two brothers returned to the cave with Adam's camera.

"You kids must really like it in there," said the guard, scratching his head in puzzlement.

This time, when they got to the smokey cavern, there was no sign of the voodoo chief.

"Maybe he's in there with the statue," suggested Sean.

"Let's go find out," said Adam. The two boys crept slowly into the large cavern.

"Look at his face now!" exclaimed Sean, pointing up at the statue. The carved wooden face was now twisted in an angry rage.

"Looks like we made him mad!" shouted Adam, who was so startled that he dropped his camera as he and Sean ran out of the cave.

At the cave's entrance, the boys received quite a shock. There stood the guard with the little voodoo chief!

"It's him!" shouted Sean. "But who is he?"

"This is my son," said the guard. "Robert, why don't you take that mask off and explain."

The "chief" slowly removed his mask, revealing himself to be a young boy, about Adam's size and age.

"I'm sorry," said Robert. "I didn't mean any harm. I live here at the hotel with my dad, and when things get a little boring I sometimes dress up like this, and try to make kids like you believe in the old legends. I snuck in and out of the cave through a back opening, so my dad wouldn't see me."

"But what about the statue's face?" asked Sean.

"The statue has three removable heads," explained Robert. "Each time you left, I changed the head to one with a new expression."

Suddenly, Adam remembered that he dropped his camera in the cave.

"Come on, Sean," he said. "Let's go back and get my camera. At least we won't have to worry about any voodoo magic this time!"

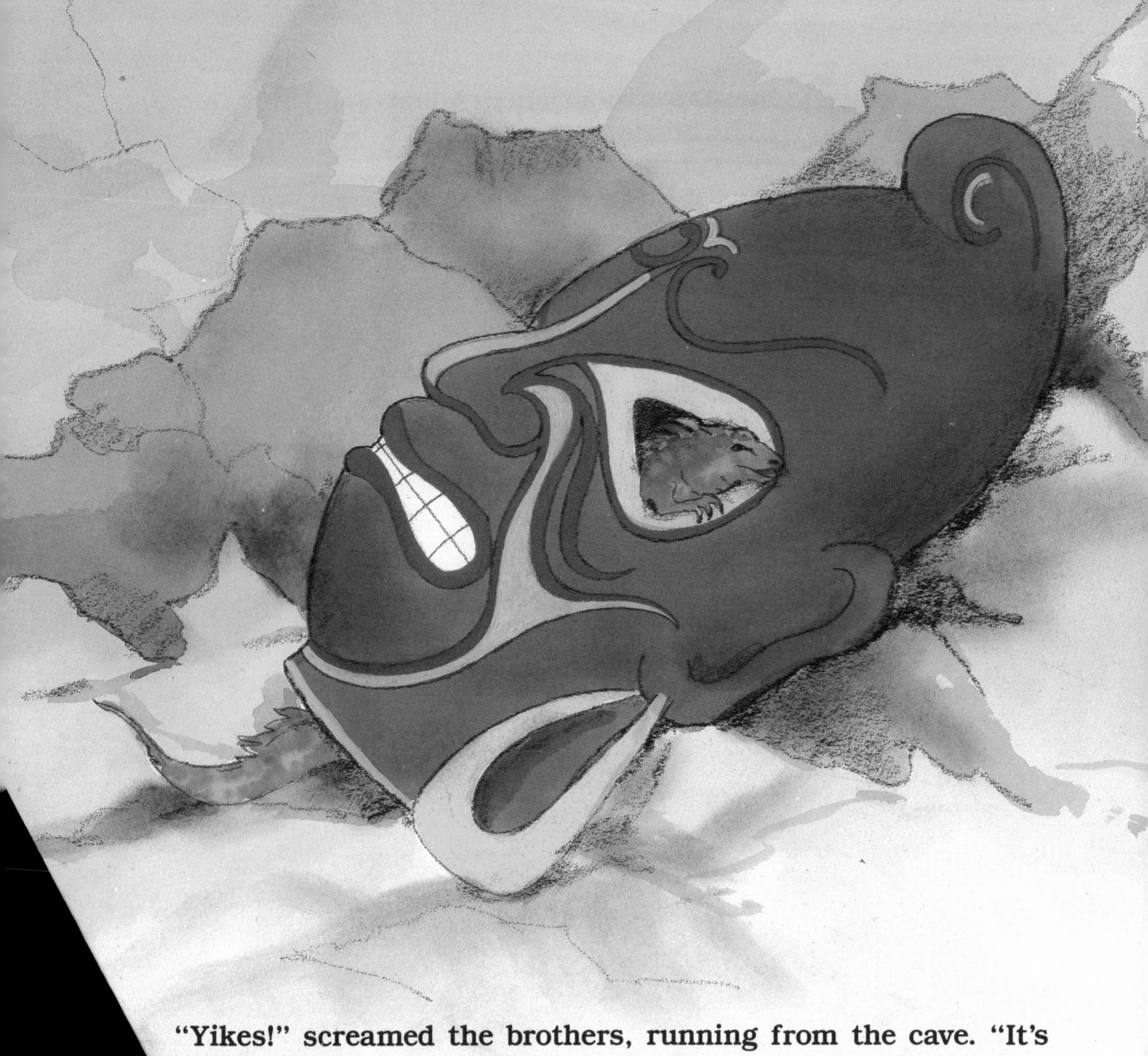

"Yikes!" screamed the brothers, running from the cave. "It's
alive! It's alive!"

Back in the cave, a lizard poked its sleepy head out through one
the statue's eyes as if he were wondering what all the noise
about.

They returned to the statue room where Adam found his camera. But when they looked up at the statue, its head was gone!

"Oh, there it is in the corner on the floor," said Sean.

Suddenly, the head with the angry expression began moving, all by itself!

of
was